W9-AUJ-878

www.enchantedlionbooks.com
First American Edition published in 2011 by Enchanted Lion Books, 20 Jay Street, Studio M-18, Brooklyn, NY 11201
 Originally published in French by Albin Michel Jeunesse, 22 rue Huyghens, 75014 Paris under the title *Pomelo grandit.* Translated by Claudia Bedrick.
A CIP record is on file with the Library of Congress. ISBN 978-1-59270-111-7
Printed in December 2010 byToppan Leefung Printing Limited,
Jin Ju Guan Li Qu, Da Ling Shan Town, Dongguan, PRC.

Ramona Badescu   Benjamin Chaud

Pomelo Begins to Grow

ENCHANTED LION BOOKS
NEW YORK

As Pomelo went on his way one morning, he passed an ant, some potatoes, a pebble, a bunch of strawberries and his favorite dandelion.

Curiously enough, his dandelion seemed surprisingly small.

As small as these
strawberries?

This pebble?

Or this teeny
tiny potato?

Not to mention this miniscule ant?

Pomelo thinks it's time to do a little measuring.

Hey, look at that…

he's grown!

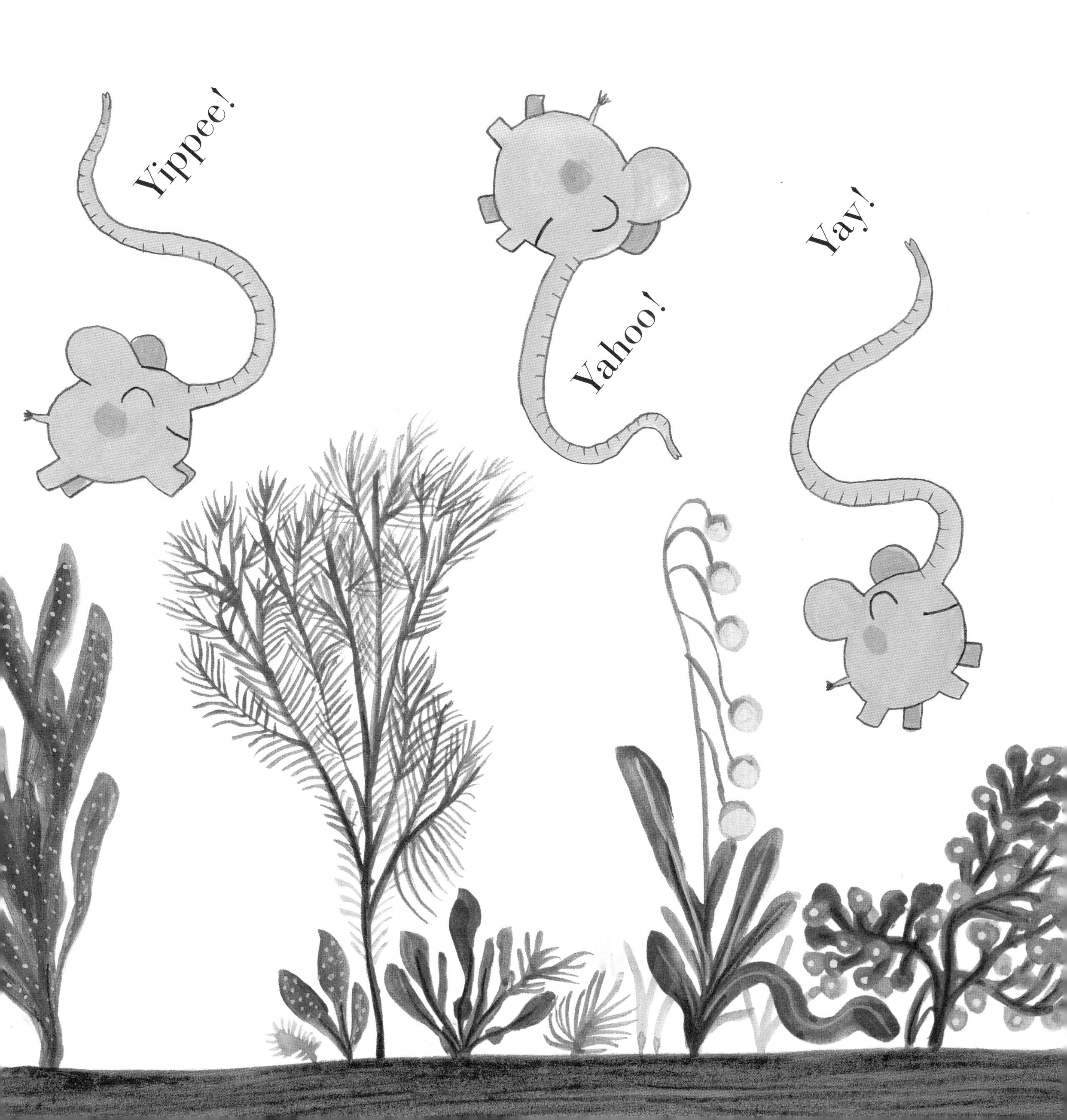
Yippee!
Yahoo!
Yay!

All at once, Pomelo feels
the super-hyper-extra force of the cosmos
spreading through him. And maybe
something even stronger than that!

He wants to do something
bigger than he's ever done before.

But wait…what's this? Is he
already too big for his
world?

And besides, doesn't he have to be medium before he gets big?

Well, yes…
but would that be
medium medium,
medium big,
big medium,
or just plain
medium?

Pomelo will have
to wait and see
as he grows
little by little.

He's a little worried that
he won't grow equally all over.

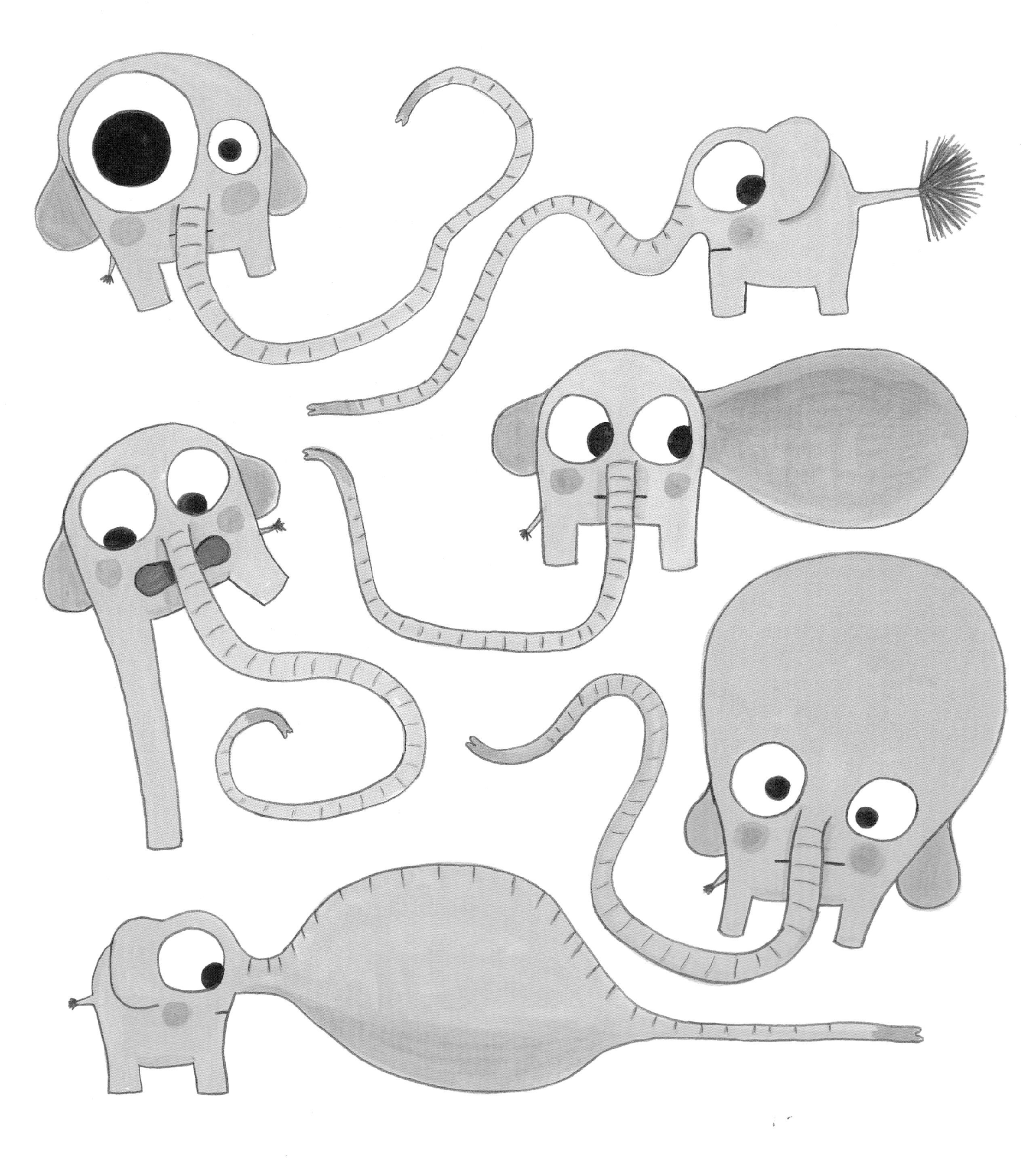

And he wonders what has to happen on the inside for him to grow on the outside.

He also asks himself if he will turn gray as he grows up?

And then there's the question if growing up means growing old?

And does growing old mean growing wise like his friend Gantok the turtle?

Does everyone in the world grow at the same speed, or do some grow more quickly than others?

Could it turn out that one day Pomelo is the biggest of all?

Hmm… could this story even go on long enough for that to happen?

Pomelo needs to make sure
he doesn't grow beyond
the edges of the page.

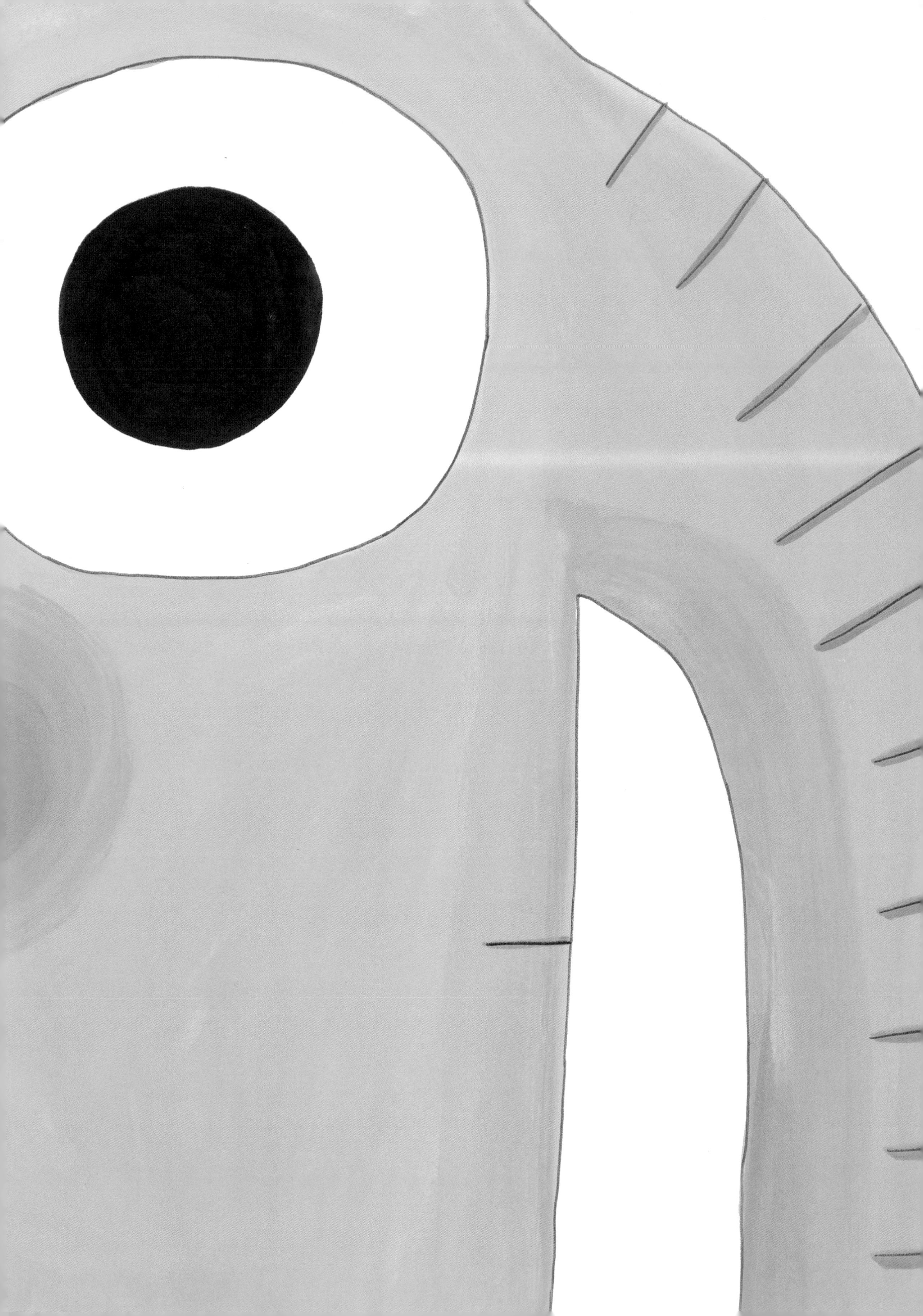

But seriously, does
growing up mean
one has to stop
clowning around?

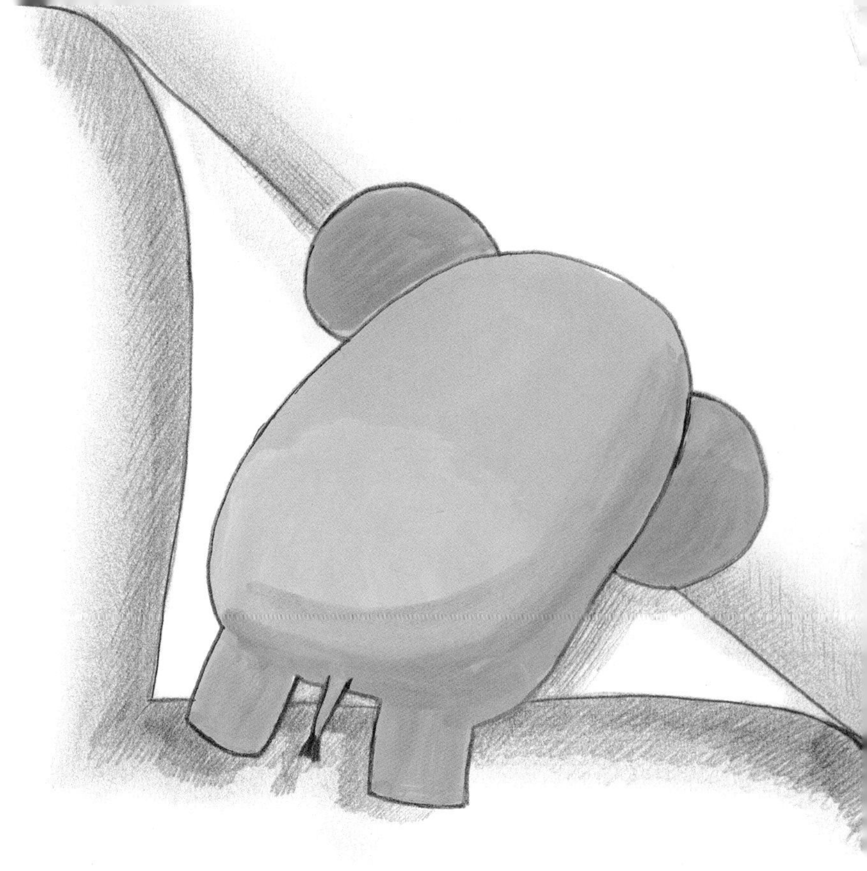

Pomelo is impatient
to turn the page...

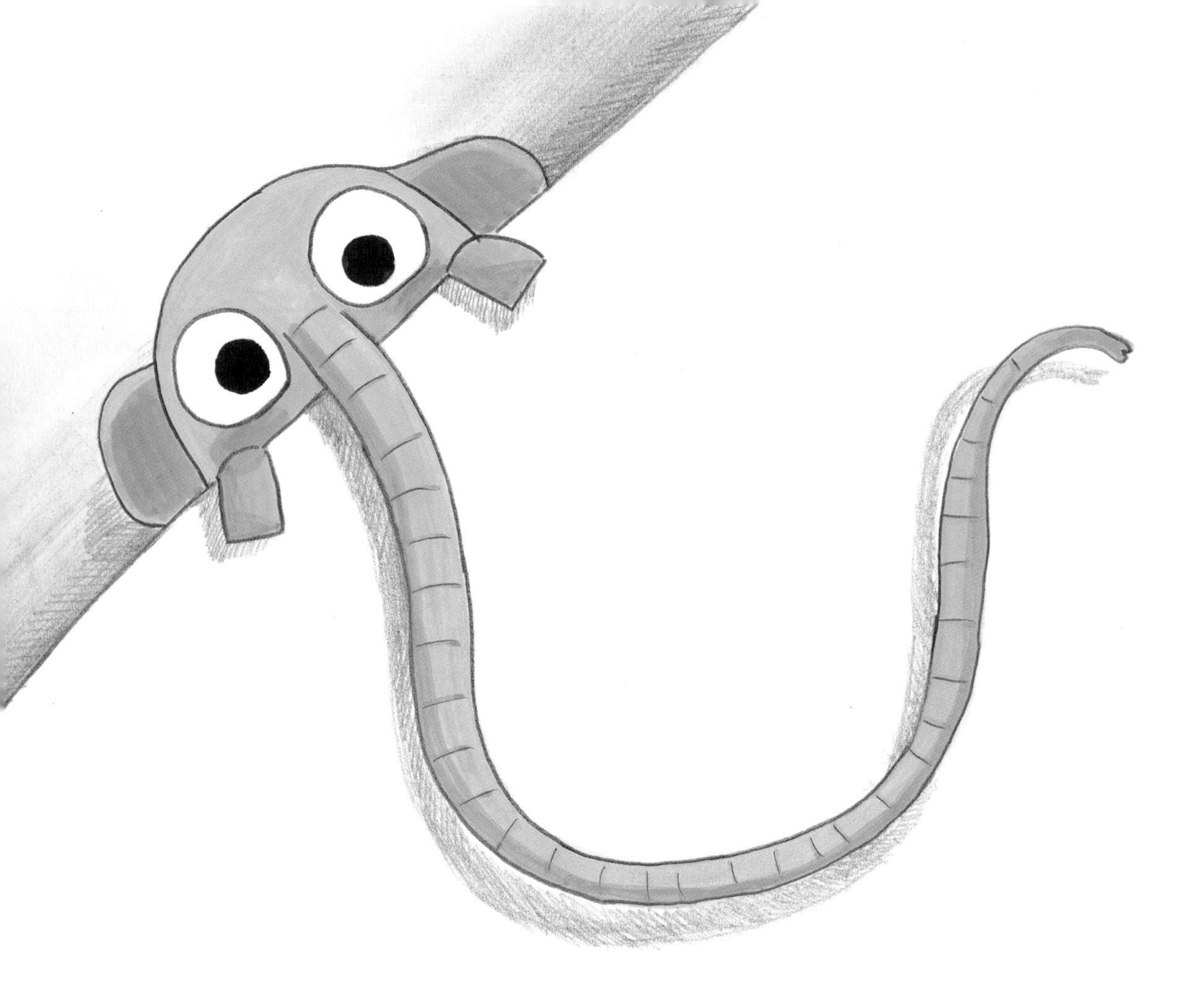

to see what comes next.

Could it be that one day he will do something he hasn't even thought of yet?

He wonders whether he will be allowed
to do whatever he wants when he is

completely
grown
up.

And will he still have to do the things that he doesn't want to do at all?

Pomelo begins to forget what it was like
to be really little.

He also begins to find little ones a bit annoying
at times…

and adults too.

But growing up is also beginning to like things he didn't like before.

And making surprising discoveries, such as it's not only round, sweet, sugary things that taste good.

Growing up is learning to make choices.

(Between running and eating, for example)

And having new experiences.

Sometimes Pomelo has the feeling that he's finally understood everything…

but it's probably just a feeling.

He would like to know what everyone
in the whole world knows.

As well as everything that everyone doesn't know.

There's no question, he want's to know more.

Such as, if a garden elephant really grows all
by himself, or if everyone is connected somehow.

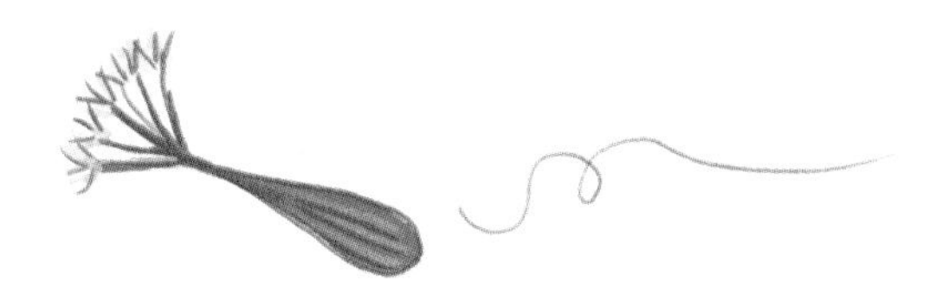

And if in beginning to grow up he has
forgotten something along the way already.

But growing up also
means that when
old fears return
you are able

…to laugh at them.

Pomelo is no longer afraid of leaving his garden.
He has discovered that growing up means learning
to say "goodbye" and being able to hear
others say it too.

Pomelo still wonders
about many things, but
now he feels big enough
for a big adventure.

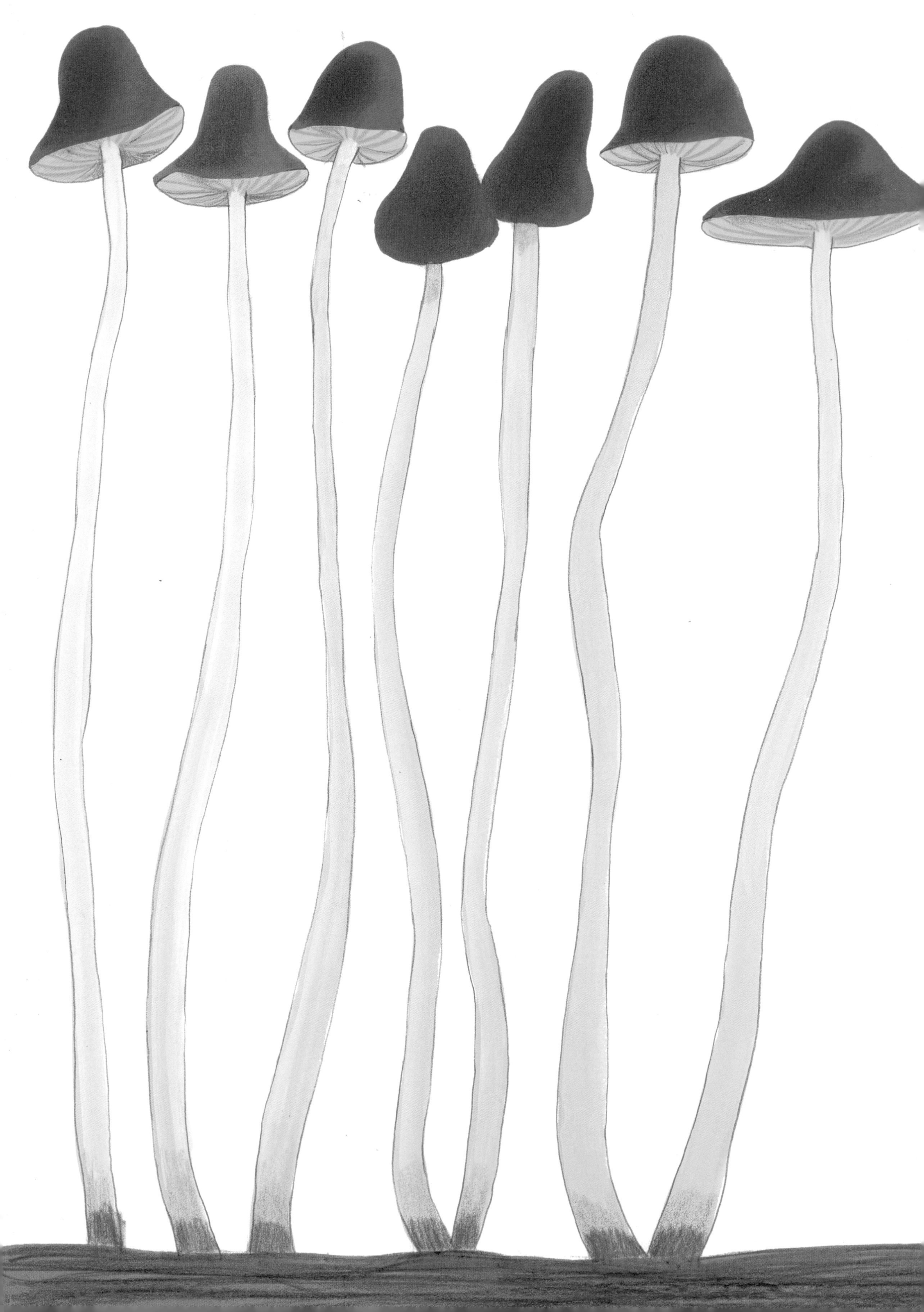